MUD
MASK

For Zoë Van Gunten —— Brian

For Nika & Ruby & Keke —— Jason

WWW.McSWEENEYS.NET

COPYRIGHT © 2012 BRIAN McMULLEN & JASON JÄGEL

McSWEENEY'S IS A PRIVATELY HELD COMPANY WITH WILDLY FLUCTUATING RESOURCES.

ALL RIGHTS RESERVED, INCLUDING THE RIGHT OF REPRODUCTION IN WHOLE OR IN PART, IN ANY FORM.

McSWEENEY'S McMULLENS WILL PUBLISH GREAT NEW BOOKS —— AND NEW EDITIONS OF

OUT-OF-PRINT CLASSICS —— FOR INDIVIDUALS AND FAMILIES OF ALL KINDS.

McSWEENEY'S McMULLENS AND COLOPHON ARE COPYRIGHT © 2012 McSWEENEY'S & McMULLENS.

PRINTED IN CHINA BY SHANGHAI OFFSET · ISBN: 978-1-936-365-83-8

THIS IS JASON AND BRIAN'S FIRST BOOK FOR CHILDREN.

McSWEENEY'S
McMULLENS

TO REACH
THE LEGS

I TURNED
THE KEY

AND CLIMBED
THE STAIRS

TO THE LADDER

TO THE
ROPE

UP UP UP
UP UP UP UP

AND UP
AND UP UP
AND UP

AND UP

AND
DOWN

DOWN
DOWN
DOWN
DOWN

AND RAN
AND LEAPT

AND FOUND
THE CLIFF

TO REACH
THE ARMS

HANG GLIDER

For Nika & Ruby & Keke ——Jason

For Zoë Van Gunten ——Brian

WWW.McSWEENEYS.NET

COPYRIGHT © 2012 JASON JÄGEL & BRIAN McMULLEN

McSWEENEY'S IS A PRIVATELY HELD COMPANY WITH WILDLY FLUCTUATING RESOURCES,
ALL RIGHTS RESERVED, INCLUDING THE RIGHT OF REPRODUCTION IN WHOLE OR IN PART, IN ANY FORM.
McSWEENEY'S McMULLENS WILL PUBLISH GREAT NEW BOOKS —— AND NEW EDITIONS OF
OUT-OF-PRINT CLASSICS —— FOR INDIVIDUALS AND FAMILIES OF ALL KINDS.
McSWEENEY'S McMULLENS AND COLOPHON ARE COPYRIGHT © 2012 McSWEENEY'S & McMULLENS.
PRINTED IN CHINA BY SHANGHAI OFFSET · ISBN: 978-1-936-365-83-8
THIS IS BRIAN AND JASON'S FIRST BOOK FOR CHILDREN.

McSWEENEY'S
McMULLENS